For my henchmen:
Rachel, Samuel,
and Matthew

Special thanks to Linda,
Andrea, Jessie, April,
John, and Dave

Requests for permission to make copies of
any part of the work should be submitted
online at www.harcourt.com/contact
or mailed to the following address:
Permissions Department, Harcourt, Inc.,
6277 Sea Harbor Drive, Orlando,
Florida 32887-6777.

www.HarcourtBooks.com

Library of Congress
Cataloging-in-Publication Data
McClements, George.
Baron von Baddie and the ice ray
incident/George McClements.
p.   cm.

Summary: When Baron von Baddie defeats his nemesis,
Captain Kapow, he discovers that it is not as much fun to create
chaos and engage in bad behavior if no one tries to stop him.
[1. Heroes—Fiction.   2. Behavior—Fiction.   3. Humorous stories.]   I. Title.
PZ7.M1325Bar   2008
[E]—dc22   2007021427
ISBN 978-0-15-206138-8

First edition
A C E G H F D B

Manufactured in China

The illustrations in this book were created using mixed-media collage.
The display and text type were set in Golgotha.
Color separations by Colourscan Co. Pte. Ltd., Singapore
Manufactured by SNP Leefung Printers Limited, China
Production supervision by Christine Witnik

Designed by April Ward and Jennifer Kelly

the neck
bone...

George McClements

BARON von BADDIE

and the

ICE RAY INCIDENT

Harcourt, Inc.

Orlando Austin New York San Diego London

Baron von Baddie was a genius.

An **EVIL** genius.

Captain Kapow always made
sure the Baron had time to think
about his actions.

In jail.

But all the Baron ever thought about
was his next invention—and escaping.

Then one day, during a
routine **ICE RAY** experiment,
the unthinkable happened.

The Baron couldn't believe his eyes.

He had actually caught Captain Kapow.

Baron von Baddie had WON!

No one could stop him now.

He could do ANYTHING
he wanted.

The first week he...

built a new
robot...

changed
Tuesday to
Wednesday...

and ate a lot
of doughnuts.

The second week he...

built another
robot...

changed
Friday to
Thursday...

and ate some
more doughnuts.

The third week he...

stopped building
robots...

missed his
birthday, so
he changed the days back...

and got sick of doughnuts.

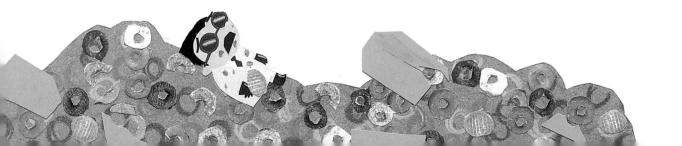

The Baron had a stunning revelation.

He missed Captain Kapow!

What was the point of creating chaos
if no one was trying to stop you?

The Baron rushed back to his lab
and spent the night building...

The Captain sprang into action,
catching the Baron and
smashing the ray.

Then he dropped the Baron at his home away from home.

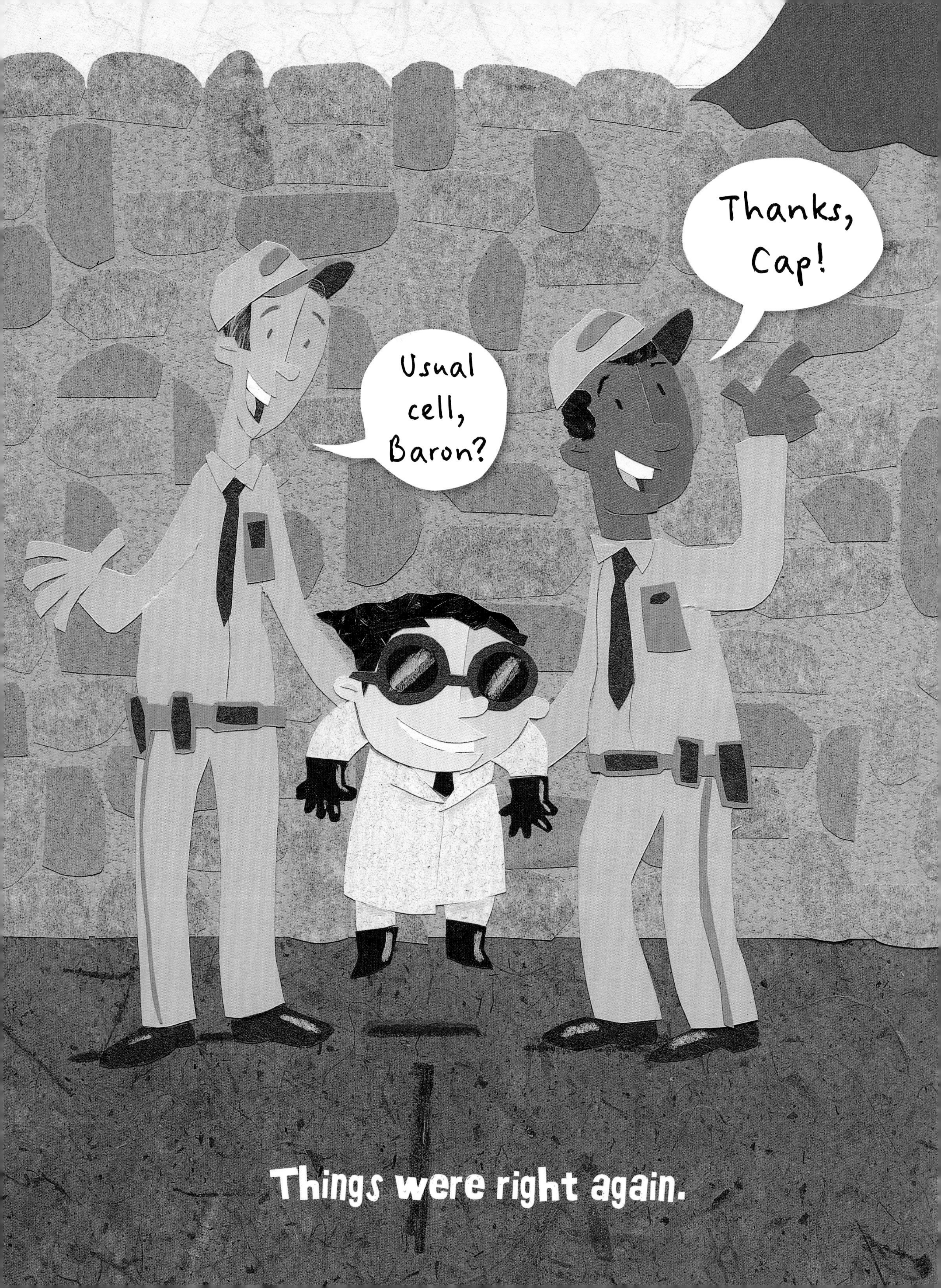

Things were right again.

The Baron even took time to
think about his actions.

And he decided not to break out.

For a whole three hours.

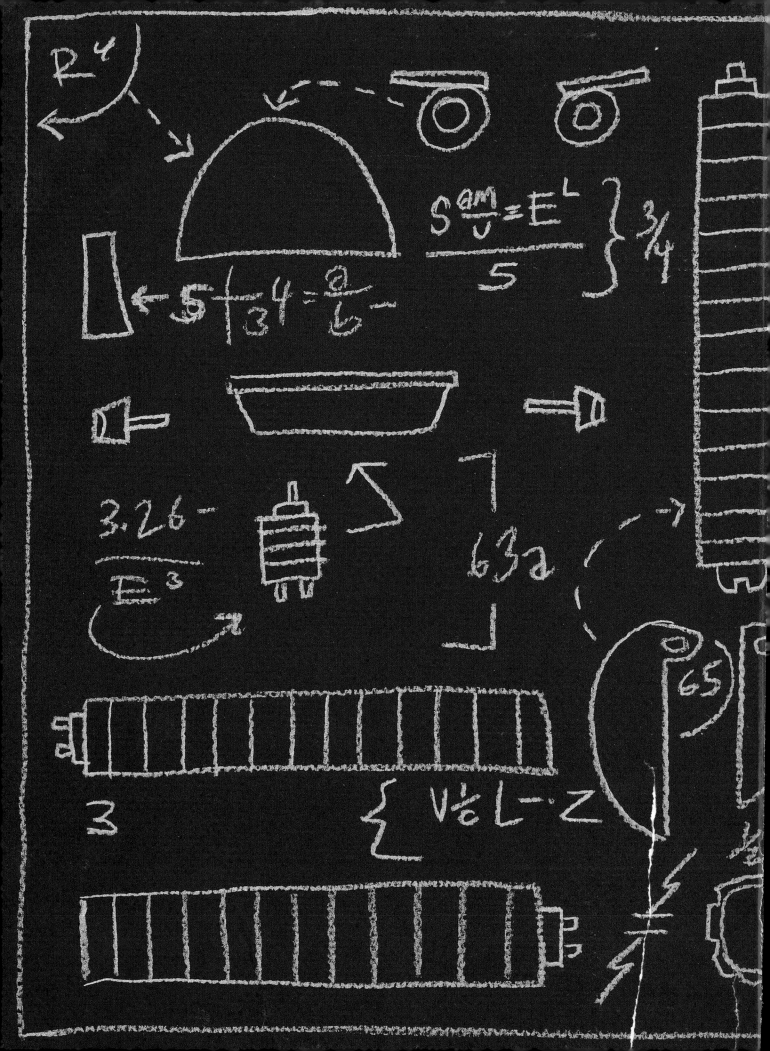